GOING TO GRANDMA'S

AROUND THE WORLD

Written by:
LENORE PAXTON
PHILLIP SIADI

Illustrated by:
JULIUS FARAGO

I love my puppy,
I like my toys,

I like my school, all the girls and boys...

But there's one thing that I like most of all,
and that's when I visit my Grandma!

I like watching TV

and going out to eat.

I like going shopping

CHOCOLATE   CANDY

I CE CREAM   POP

and getting yummy treats!

But there's one thing
that I like most of all,
and that's when I visit my Grandma!

She buys me stuff

and makes good things to eat.

She reads me stories.
(Boy, I think that's neat!)

She hugs and kisses, and I must insist...
Grandma is Number 1 on my list.

Grandmas don't get angry,
Grandpas don't get mad.
They make me happy when I feel sad.

So the one thing that
I like best of all is
going to visit Grandma!

I love my Grandma, as you can see, and
the happiest time is when my mom tells me
to put on my sweater and jump in the car
'cause we're going to visit
Grandma!

In **ITALY**,
Grandma is
"NONA"

TI VOLGLIO BENE,
NONA
(TEE VO-leo BAY-nay, NO-nah)

JA CIE KOCHAM, BABCIA
(YA CHA KOH-HAM, BOB-CHA)

In **JAPAN** Grandma is "OBA SAN"

BOKU-WA OBASAN-GA DAISUKI DESU
(BOH-KOO-WAH OH-BAH-SAHN-GA DYE-SKEE-DES)

In **FRANCE** Grandma is "GRANDMAMAN"

JE VOUS AIME, GRANDMAMAN
(JEH VOO ZEM, GRAHN-MAMA)

In **ARABIC** Grandma is "SITAY"

ANAHIBIC, SITAY

(AH-NUH-HIH-BIC, SIH-TAY)

In **GERMANY** Grandma is "OMA"

ICH LIEBE
DIECH, OMA
(ICK LEE-BUH DEEK,
OH-MAH)

In **HUNGARY** Grandma is "NAGYMAMA"

NAGYON SZERETLEK, NAGYMAMA
(NAH-JEE-OHN SER-ET-LEK, NAHJ-MAH-MAH)

In **SPANISH** Grandma is "ABUELA"

YO TE AMO, ABUELA
(YOH TAY AH-MO, AH-BWAY-LAH)

Don't forget **GRANDPA** too!

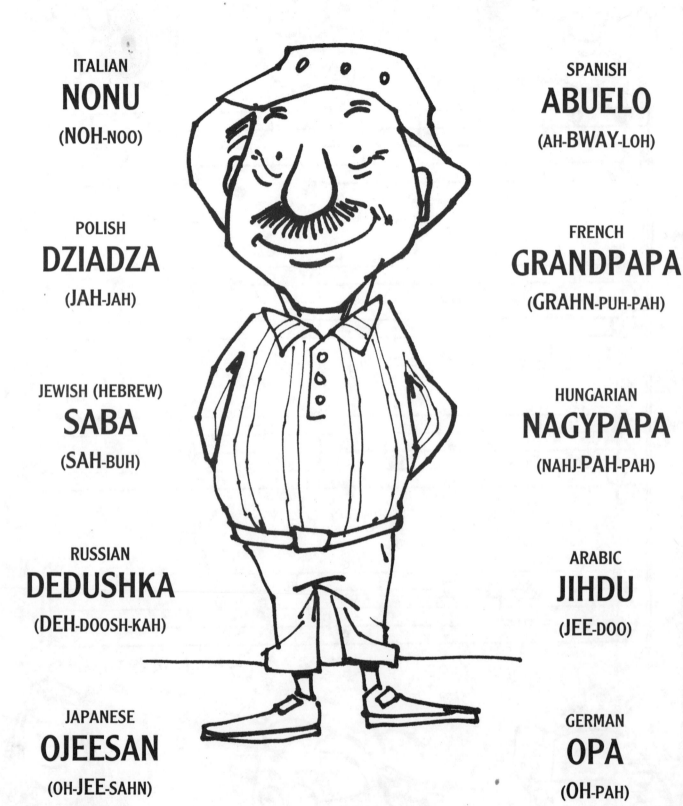

ITALIAN
NONU
(NOH-NOO)

POLISH
DZIADZA
(JAH-JAH)

JEWISH (HEBREW)
SABA
(SAH-BUH)

RUSSIAN
DEDUSHKA
(DEH-DOOSH-KAH)

JAPANESE
OJEESAN
(OH-JEE-SAHN)

SPANISH
ABUELO
(AH-BWAY-LOH)

FRENCH
GRANDPAPA
(GRAHN-PUH-PAH)

HUNGARIAN
NAGYPAPA
(NAHJ-PAH-PAH)

ARABIC
JIHDU
(JEE-DOO)

GERMAN
OPA
(OH-PAH)